THIS IS THE FARMER

NANCY TAFURI

GREENWILLOW BOOKS · NEW YORK

FOR CRISTINA!

MANY THANKS TO
HELEN AND ED GIBBONS
(MY FARMER AND WIFE)
AND TO THEIR
"WEE FARM FOR WEE FOLKS"

Watercolor inks and a black pen
were used for the full-color art.
The text type is Garamond.

Printed in Singapore
by Tien Wah Press

First Edition
10 9 8 7 6 5 4 3 2 1

Library of Congress
Cataloging-in-Publication Data

Tafuri, Nancy.
  This is the farmer / by Nancy Tafuri.
    p.   cm.
  Summary: A farmer's kiss causes an
amusing chain of events on the farm.
  ISBN 0-688-09468-6 (trade).
ISBN 0-688-09469-4 (lib. bdg.)
  [1. Farm life—Fiction.]   I. Title.
PZ7.T117Th   1994   [E]—dc20
  92-30082   CIP   AC

This is the farmer

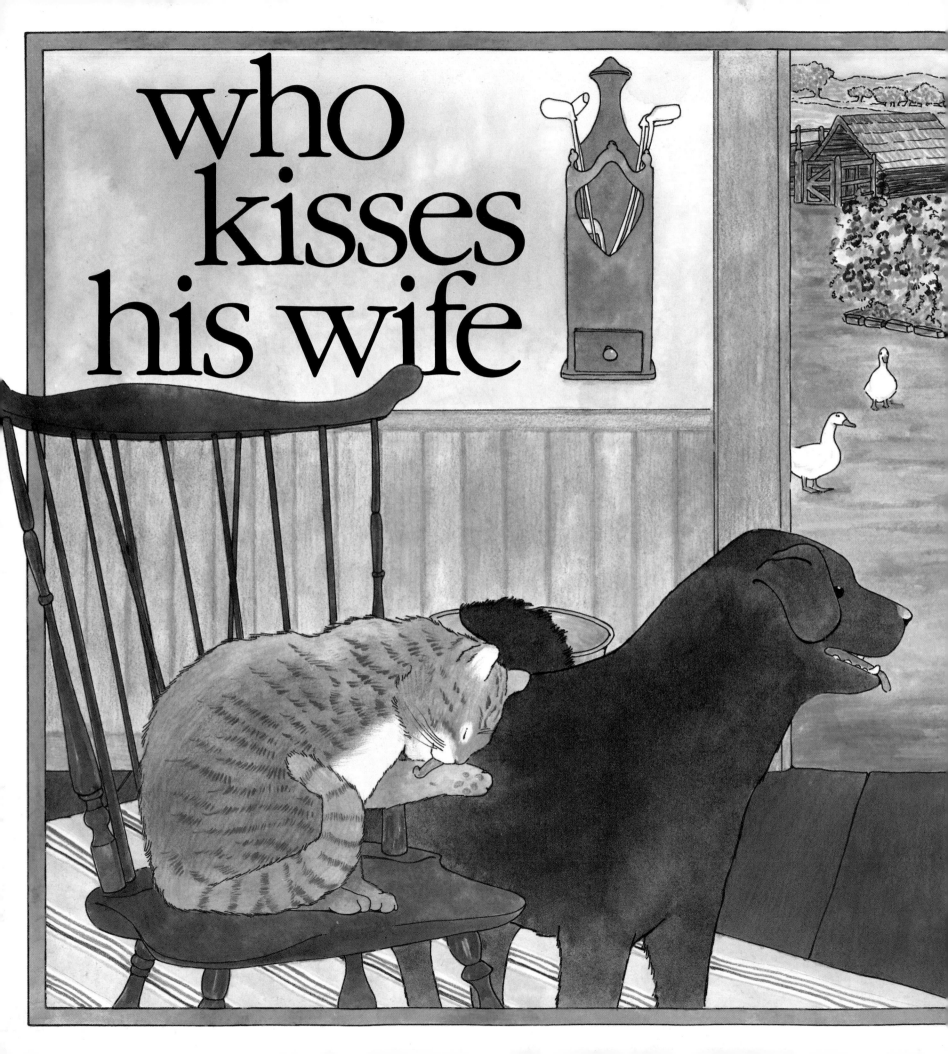

who
kisses
his wife

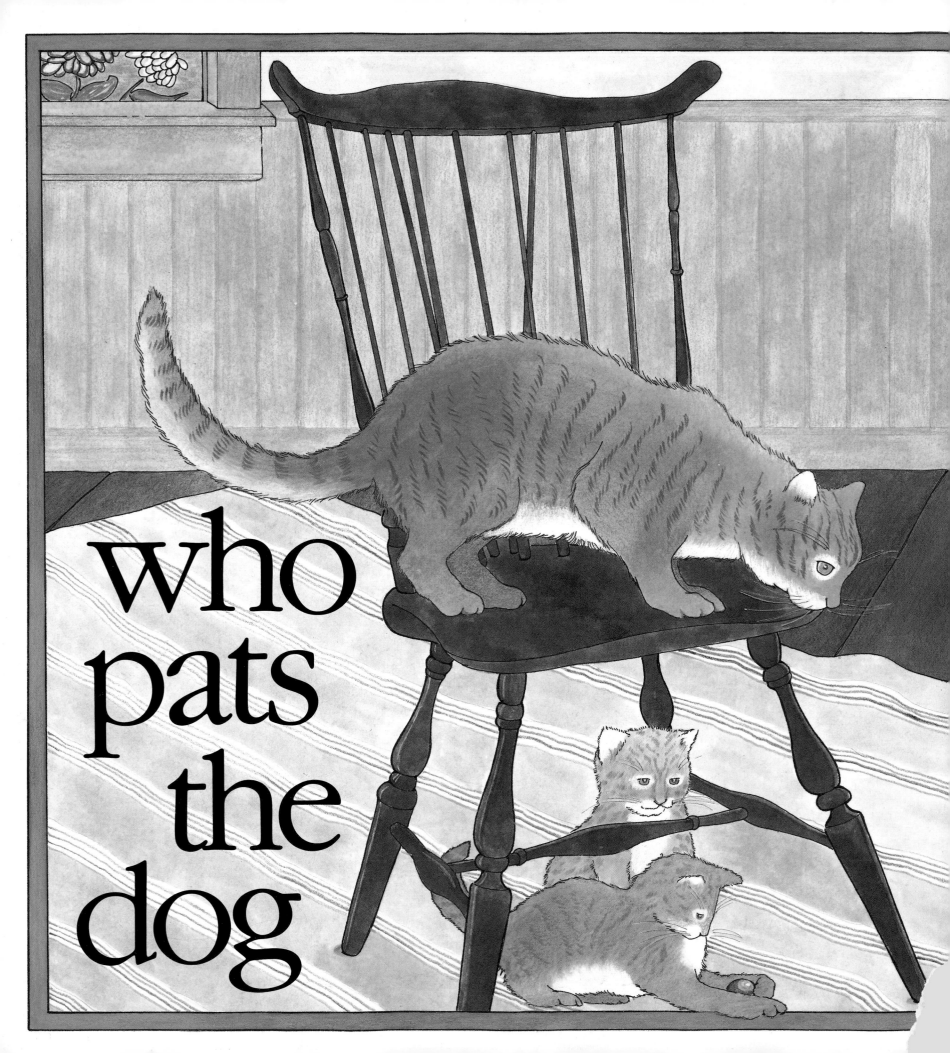

who
pats
the
dog

that scratches
a flea

that
lands
on
the cat

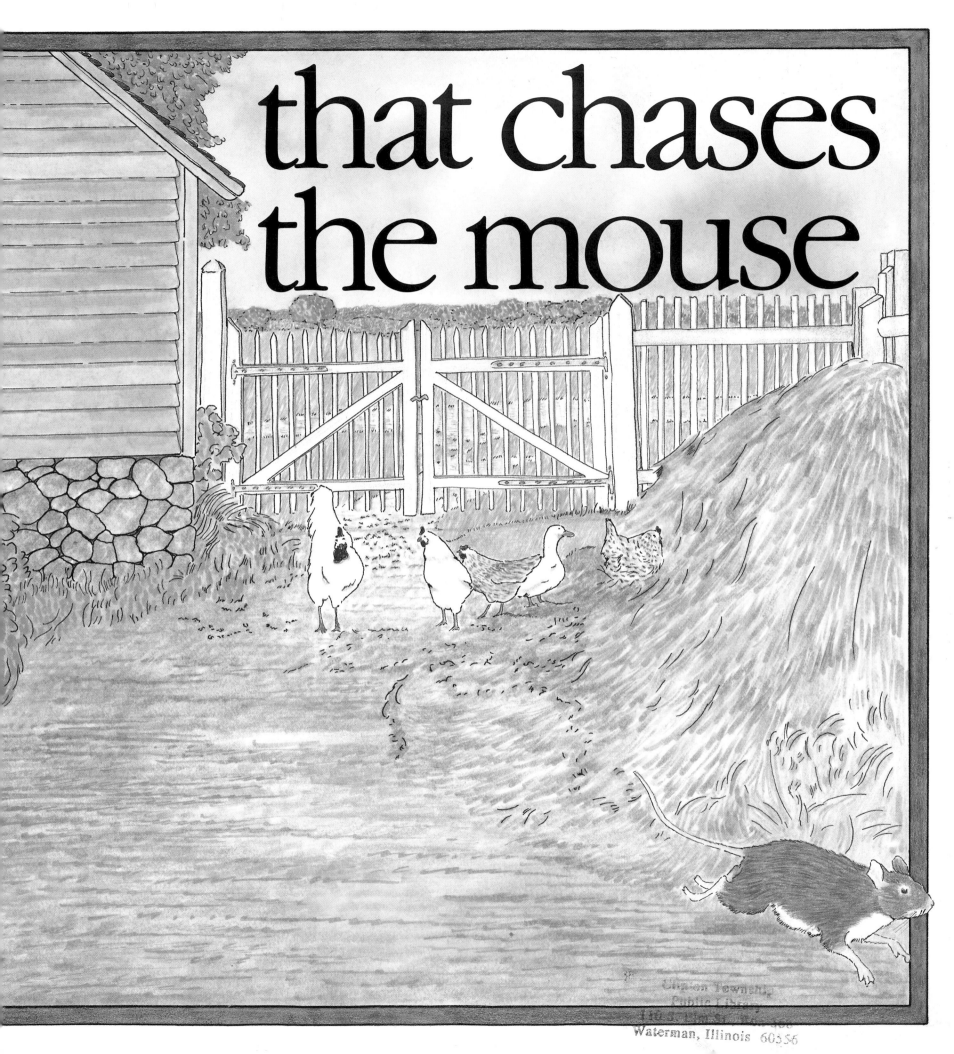

that chases
the mouse

that
startles
the
geese

that run by

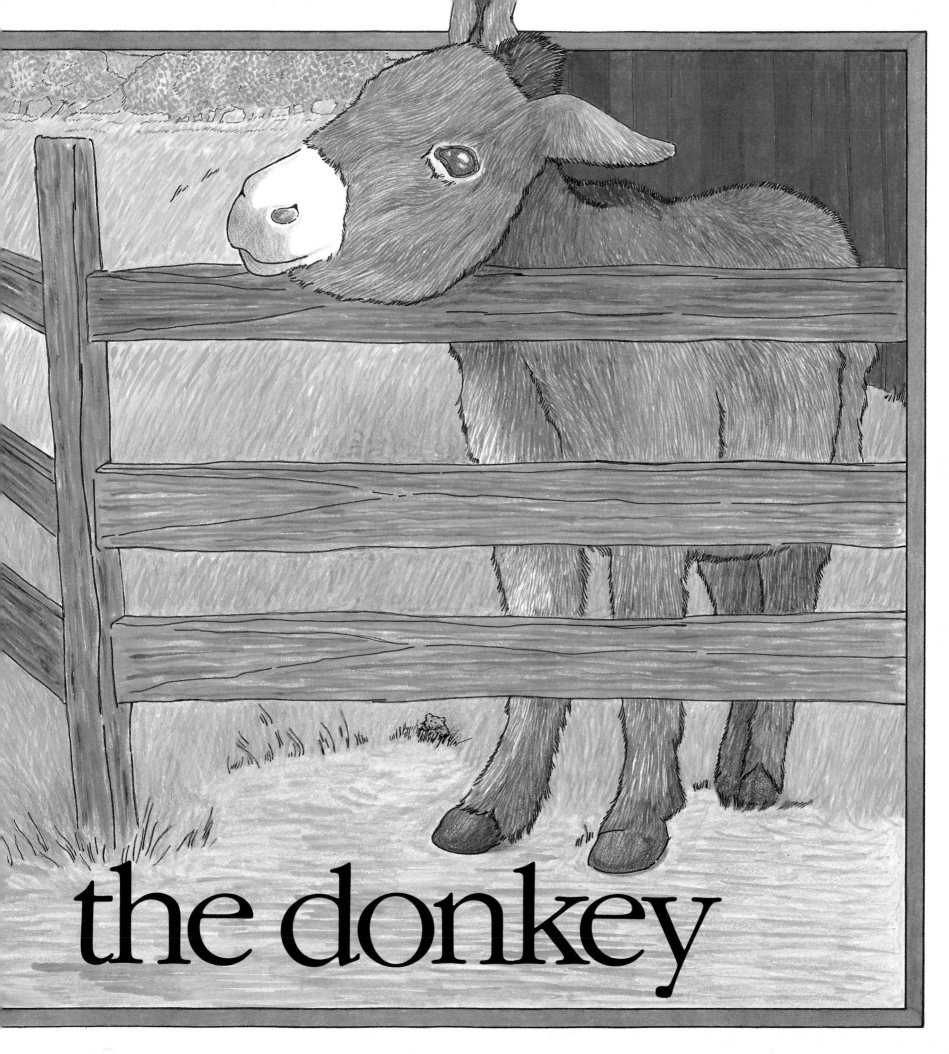

the donkey

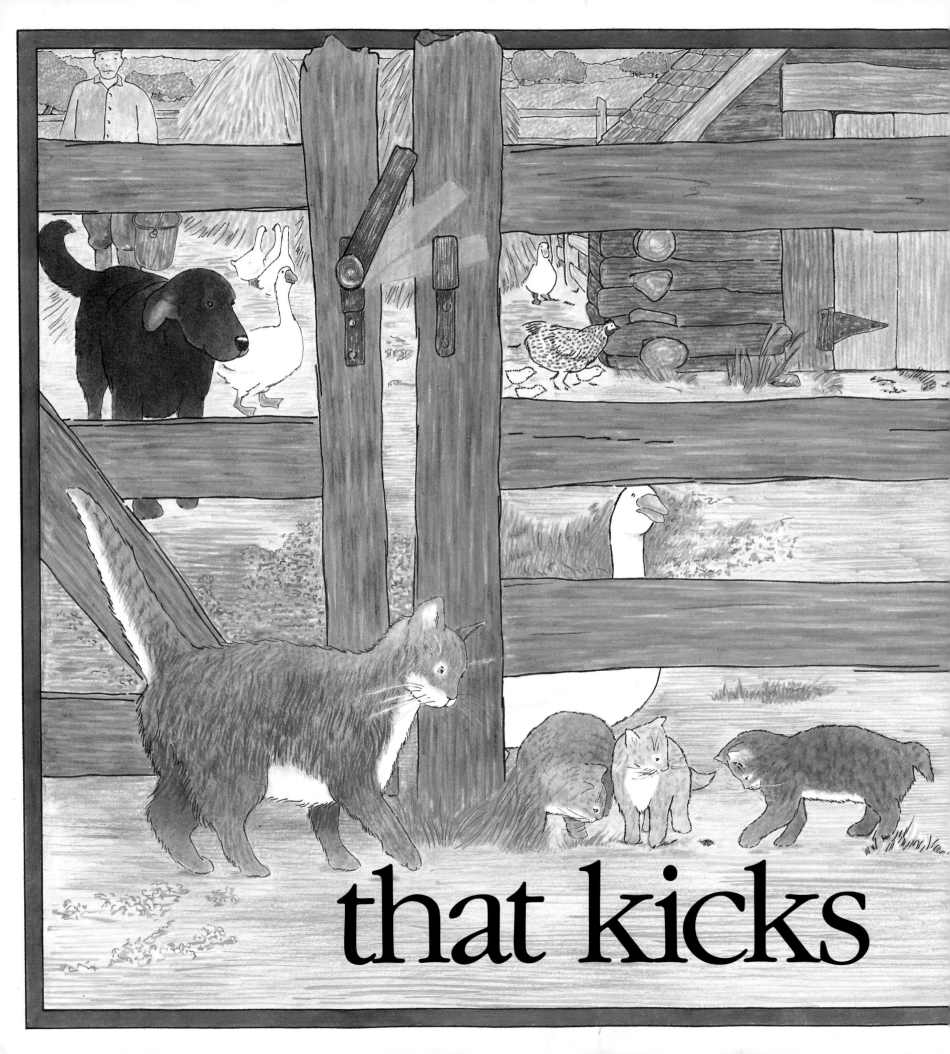

that kicks

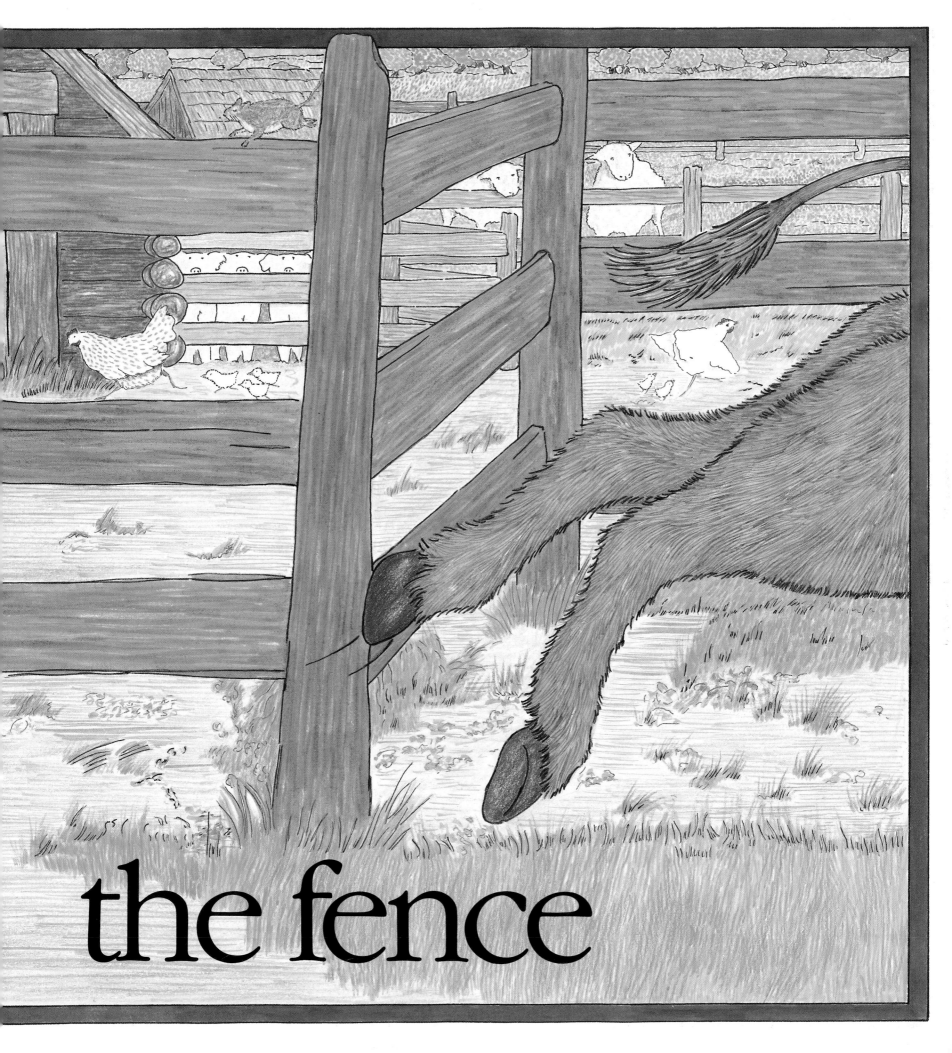

the fence

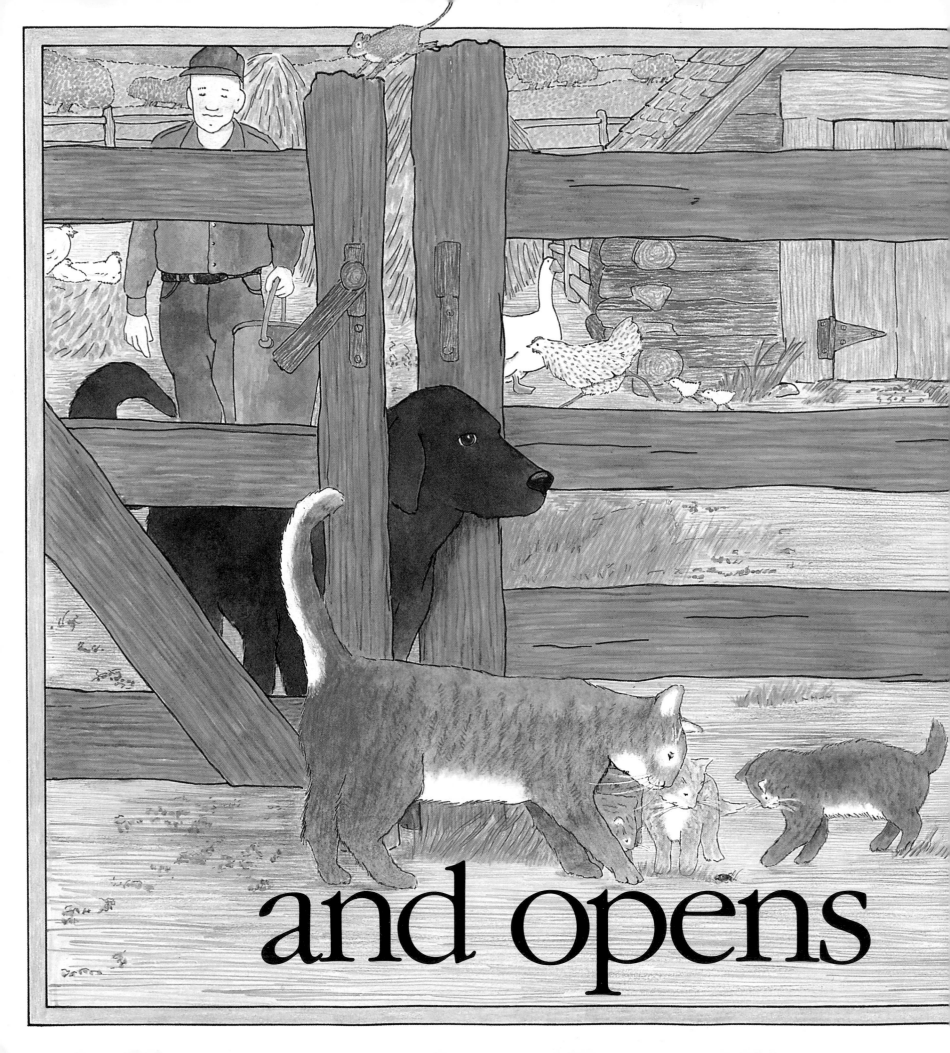

and opens

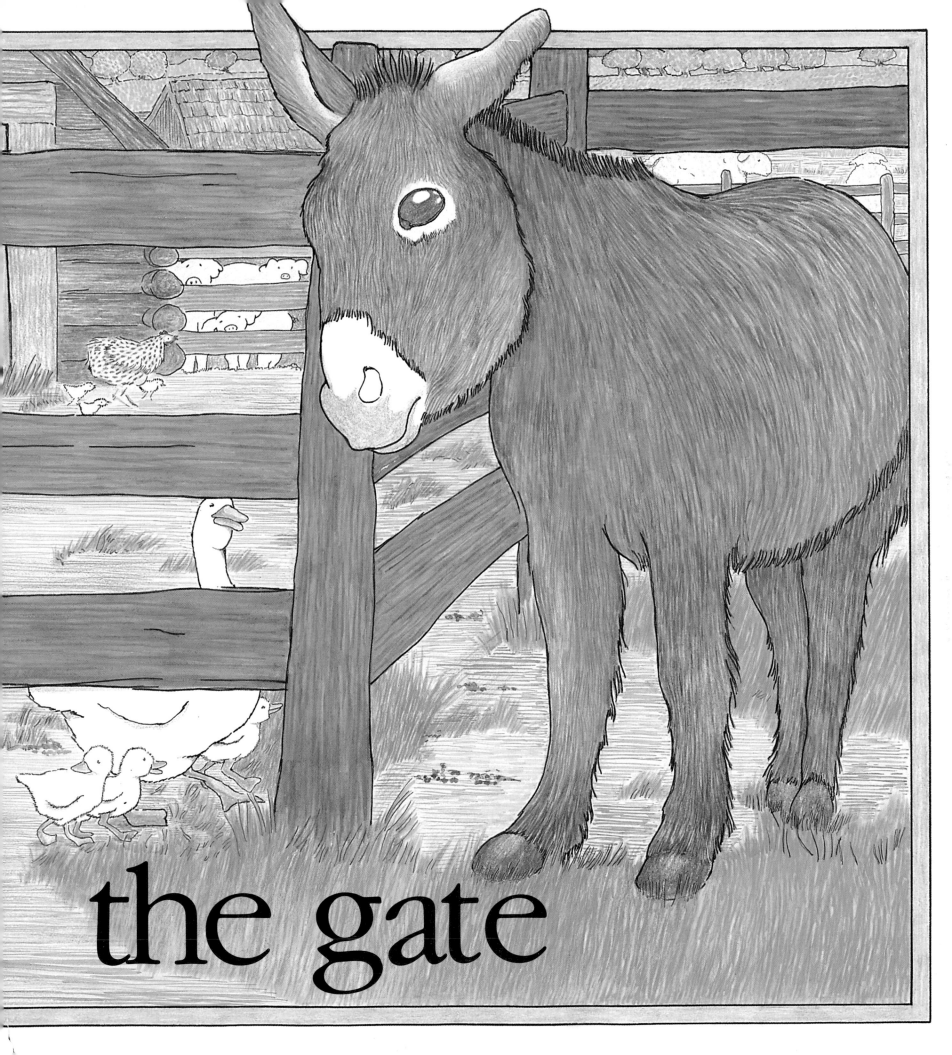

the gate

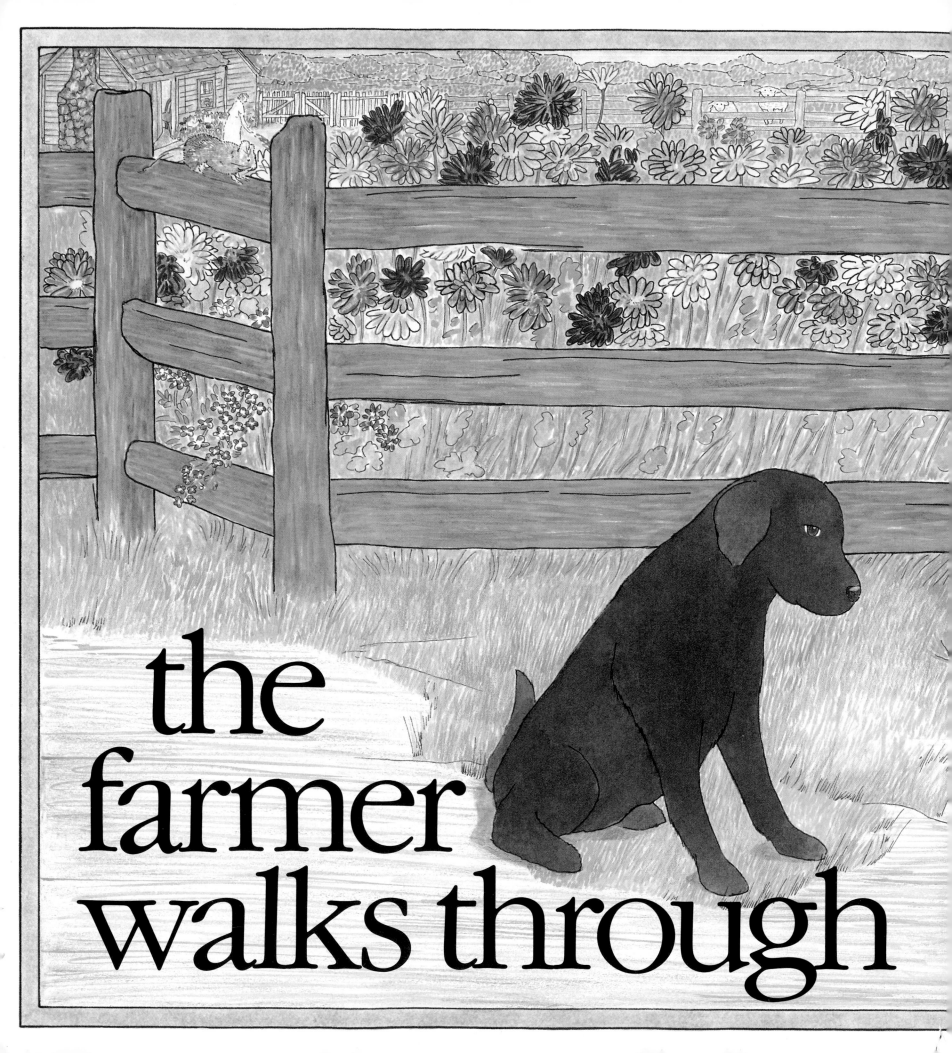

the
farmer
walks through

to
milk
the
cow!